A HARE, A HOUND
& SHY MOUSEY BROWN

To the ones who make me jump for joy –
Mark, James, Joe, and Jess—JH

For Madison, Dakota, Bailey, and Cooper—JB

An Imprint of Sterling Publishing
387 Park Avenue South
New York, NY 10016

SANDY CREEK and the distinctive Sandy Creek logo
are registered trademarks of Barnes & Noble, Inc.

Text © 2012 by Julia Hubery
Illustrations © 2012 by Jonathan Bentley

This 2013 edition published by Sandy Creek.

ISBN 978-1-4351-4729-4

Manufactured in Shenzhen, China
Lot #:
2   4   6   8   10   9   7   5   3   1
02/13

Julia Hubery &
Jonathan Bentley

A Hare a Hound &

Shy
Mousey
Brown

Sandy Creek
NEW YORK

There's a hare in the air, there's a hound on the ground,
and watching them both is shy Mousey Brown
from his hole in the wall, not making a sound,
so nobody knows that he's there.

The hare in the air
is simply astounding,
singing the spring in
with whirling and bounding.

Mousey Brown's heart
goes pitter-pat-pounding
with love for her daring and flair.

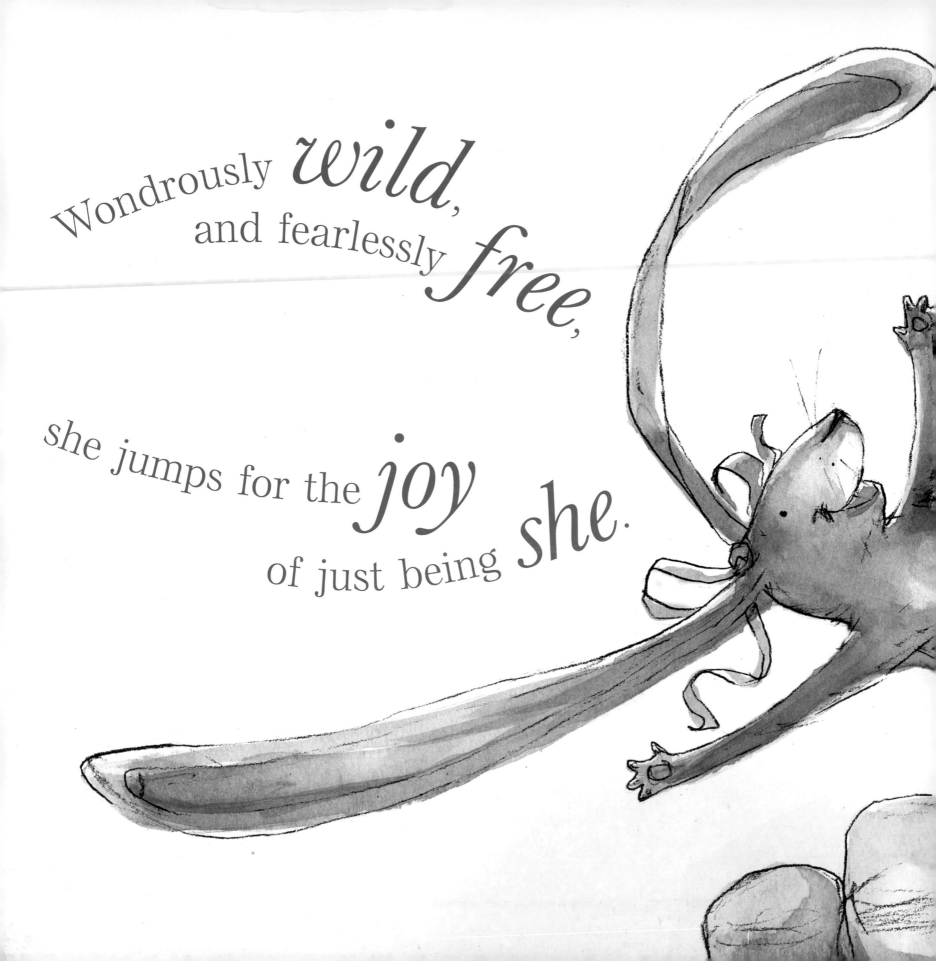

Wondrously *wild*, and fearlessly *free*,
she jumps for the *joy* of just being *she*.

"How could I hope
that she'd even see me?"
thinks poor Mousey Brown
in despair.

The daft dizzy dancer goes
laughing and leaping
right up to the hound,
who pretends to be sleeping,

but Mousey Brown knows
that he's secretly keeping
a watch on the hoppity hare.

For he knows this sly dog, he's seen him before:
he'll lie there as still as a log till he's sure
that the hare is in reach of his snappity jaws—
then he'll snatch her right out of the air!

"How can I warn her? I'm so very small!"
thinks shy Mousey Brown in his hole in the wall.

He takes a deep breath, and he leans out and bawls
in his biggest best bellow:

"Bewa

But the hare doesn't hear him,
she pats the hound's nose,
tweaks his old tail, and tickles his toes.

"Wake up, sleepy doggy,
it's springtime, you knows!"
she whispers right into his ear.

With a

leap and a **snap** and a **swipe** of his paw,

the hound on the ground
isn't there anymore.
He's up in the air
and he's boxing the hare …

with a **thud!**
and a **thwack!**

she's pinned on her back,
and quakes at his menacing stare.

Her beautiful eyes are shining with fear
as he lashes a lick up her long lovely ear.
"Gosh, you'll be ever so tasty!" he sneers …

and Mousey Brown
leaps from his lair!

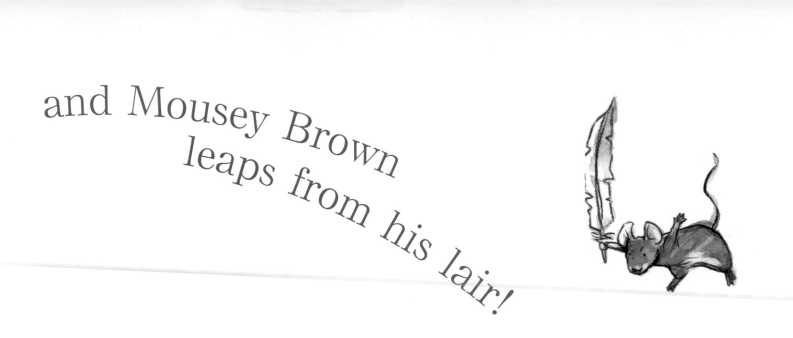

Clutching a feather, he hurls himself down
right into the ear of the huge hungry hound

and relentlessly *tickles,*
the hound into *giggles,*

wriggles

until he's wound tight in a knot with his

and can't move a whisker or hair.

Then Mousey strides out
with his feather held high,
he feels like a warrior,
tall as the sky.

He bows to the hare
with a bold twinkling eye,
and says, "Pleased to meet you,
my dear!"

"You saved me!" the hare cries.
"I'll love you forever
you bold mouseketeer,
so fearless and clever!

Come with me now,
let's go dancing together,
we've got a whole springtime
to share!"

Mousey Brown and the hare
make a curious pair,
and when they go dancing,
the neighbors all stare.

The hare doesn't notice,
Mousey Brown doesn't care ...